Karen's

D0047729

**Other books by
Ann M. Martin**

P.S. Longer Letter Later
(written with Paula Danziger)
Leo the Magnificat
Rachel Parker, Kindergarten Show-off
Eleven Kids, One Summer
Ma and Pa Dracula
Yours Turly, Shirley
Ten Kids, No Pets
With You and Without You
Me and Katie (the Pest)
Stage Fright
Inside Out
Bummer Summer

For older readers:

Missing Since Monday
Just a Summer Romance
Slam Book

THE BABY-SITTERS CLUB series
THE BABY-SITTERS CLUB mysteries
THE KIDS IN MS. COLMAN'S CLASS series
BABY-SITTERS LITTLE SISTER series
(see inside book covers for a complete listing)

Little Sister

Karen's Paper Route
Ann M. Martin

Illustrations by Susan Tang

A
LITTLE APPLE
PAPERBACK

SCHOLASTIC INC.
New York Toronto London Auckland Sydney

ISBN 0-590-06595-5

12 11 10 9 8 7 6 5 4 3 2 1   8 9/9 0 1/0 2/0

Printed in the U.S.A.   40
First Scholastic printing, May 1998

*The author gratefully acknowledges
Stephanie Calmenson
for her help
with this book.*

Karen's Paper Route

Tag, You Are It!

It was a sunny Saturday in May. My favorite kind of day.

My friends and I were outside playing a game of tree tag. In tree tag, if you are touching a tree, you are safe from being tagged.

Hannie Papadakis had her eye on me. I was nowhere near a tree. And Hannie was it.

"You would not!" I said. "We are best friends."

"I would," she replied. "And I am going to get you right now."

She raced after me and tapped my arm.

"Tag, you are it!" she called.

Boo. Oh, well. I really do not mind being it. I like running after my friends and trying to tag them. I love running and playing.

My name is Karen Brewer. I am seven years old. I have blonde hair, blue eyes, and freckles. I wear glasses. I wear my blue pair when I am reading. I wear my pink pair when I am playing tag and doing just about everything else. (Well, not sleeping.)

I saw David Michael out of the corner of my eye and headed in his direction. He saw me coming and raced to the closest tree before I could reach him.

Boo. Big boo! I like tagging my seven-year-old stepbrother. I would just have to try again later.

Callie and Keith Bates were racing by me, giggling. (They are twins and they are only

2

four.) I ran to catch them. They grabbed on to each other and started screaming as soon as I got near them.

"You need to touch a tree to be safe, not each other!" I said.

That made them scream even louder. They started hopping up and down instead of running toward a tree. I decided not to tag them even though I was close enough. I was afraid whoever I tagged might start to cry.

I spun around fast and reached out.

"Tag, you are it!" I called.

I did it! David Michael was trying to slip past me, but I got him.

"Karen and David Michael! It is time to come inside for lunch," called Kristy.

Kristy is my big stepsister. She is thirteen years old and the best sister ever.

I was having fun playing tag, but I was also getting hungry.

"See you later!" I called to my friends.

"I am going to visit my relatives later. We

are staying overnight," said Hannie. "So I will see you on Monday."

"Have a good time," I replied.

I followed David Michael inside. I knew a delicious lunch was waiting for us.

Big House, Big Lunch

Saturday lunches at the big house are the best. We bring out all the leftovers from the week and line them up on our kitchen table. Then everyone gets a plate and starts filling it.

This is what I took: tuna salad, cold spaghetti, pickles, corn chips, guacamole. Does that sound weird? It was not. It was an excellent lunch.

The reason we have so much food is that there are so many of us. Right now there are nine people at the big house. And that is only part of my family. I will tell you the story of my family, in case you want to know.

A long time ago, when I was very young, my family was just Mommy, Daddy, Andrew, and me. (Andrew is my little brother. He is four going on five.) We all lived together right here in this big house, in Stoneybrook, Connecticut.

Then Mommy and Daddy got divorced. My one small family split up, and then it grew. This is how.

Mommy moved out with Andrew and me to a little house not far away. Then she met a very nice man named Seth. She and Seth got married and now Seth is my stepfather. Seth brought along his dog, Midgie, and his cat, Rocky.

We all lived together in the little house with Emily Junior, my pet rat, and Bob, Andrew's hermit crab. That is, until recently. You see, Seth had to move to Chicago for a few months to take a very good job. Mommy, Andrew, and I went with him. But

I missed Stoneybrook so much I came back. So for now, Mommy, Seth, and Andrew live in Chicago, and I live here in the big house.

The big house is where Daddy stayed after the divorce. (It is the house he grew up in.) He also met someone very nice and got married again. She is Elizabeth and now she is my stepmother. Elizabeth was married once before and has four children. They are my stepbrothers and stepsister. They are David Michael, Kristy, Sam and Charlie. (Sam and Charlie are so old they are in high school.)

My other sister is Emily Michelle, who is two and a half. Daddy and Elizabeth adopted her from a faraway country called Vietnam. I love her a lot, which is why I named my rat after her.

Nannie, my stepgrandmother, also lives at the big house. She is Elizabeth's mother.

Here are the pets: They are Shannon, David Michael's big Bernese mountain dog puppy; Scout, our training-to-be-a-guide-dog puppy; Boo-Boo, Daddy's cranky old cat; Crystal Light the Second, my goldfish; and Goldfishie, Andrew's fish. When Andrew asked Goldfishie to move to Chicago, the answer was no. At least we think it was. That is why Goldfishie stayed behind.

Before the move to Chicago, Andrew and I switched houses almost every month — we spent one month at the big house, then one month at the little house. That is when I gave us our special names. I call us Andrew Two-Two and Karen Two-Two. (I thought up those names after my teacher read a book to our class. It was called *Jacob Two-Two Meets the Hooded Fang*.) I call us those names because we have two of so many things. We have two families with two mommies and two daddies. We each have two sets of toys and clothes and books. We have two bicycles, one at each house. I also have two best friends. Hannie lives across the street and one house over from the big house. Nancy Dawes lives next door to the little house.

That is my story. While I was telling it to you, I ate everything on my plate. It was very delicious. I think I need a refill.

Work, Work, Work!

I woke up on Sunday with the sun streaming through my window. It was another beautiful day.

I remembered that Hannie was not around. Nancy had said she would be busy with her family too. I decided to see what *my* family was doing.

"Is there anything special for breakfast?" I asked. On Sundays, Nannie sometimes makes pancakes or waffles. Or Daddy buys muffins and bagels.

"I am sorry, Karen," said Nannie. "I have

a rush order to fill this afternoon. I have been up since early this morning making my candies."

Nannie started a home candy-making business. She works out of the new kitchen that used to be our pantry. I should have known she had started cooking from the good, sweet smells drifting around the house.

I did not see Daddy. Maybe he was out shopping. I peeked out the window. His car was in the driveway. Then I heard papers rustling in his office. (Daddy works at home.)

Oh, well. It was a Krispy Krunchies morning. I put some strawberries on my cereal and gobbled my breakfast down.

Now it was time to have fun. Maybe Kristy would do something fun with me. I knocked on the door to her room. Kristy was tying back her hair. She looked as if she were getting ready to go somewhere.

"What are you doing today?" I asked. "Do you want to do something fun with me?"

"I would like to, Karen. But I got called yesterday for a last-minute baby-sitting job," she replied.

"Too bad," I said.

I looked for David Michael. He was not in his room. I found him in the den with Elizabeth. He was piling up papers and stapling them together.

"What are you doing?" I asked.

"I have a crash deadline," replied Elizabeth. Elizabeth works for an advertising company. I used to think her job was boring. Then she put my classmates and me into a Wacky Cracky Bubble Gum commercial. It was so much fun!

"I am helping," replied David Michael.

"Oh," I said. I slipped away.

Nannie said that Sam was at the A&P. (That is where he works.) And Charlie was driving around delivering flowers for the flower shop. (They were having a busy day and needed extra drivers.)

Hmmph. The only ones who did not have jobs were me, Emily Michelle, and our pets.

I thought about getting a job myself. It could be a good thing. Or not. Good thing. Not a good thing. Good thing. Not a good thing.

I could see it both ways.

Finally I decided not to decide. Instead I went outside to ride my bike. It was the weekend and I was going to have fun.

I had a very good time too, even without my family. I rode my bike, played with some kids in the neighborhood, and read a funny book out in the yard. So there.

But I Want It *Now*!

I had a very good day at school on Monday. I answered all my math problems right. And I won a class spelling bee. (I am a very good speller. I even won a county spelling bee once.)

After school I ate a snack, did my homework, then watched TV. (It was raining, so I did not go outside to play.)

While I was watching, I saw a commercial for Moonbeam, the new video game system. I had heard some kids talking about it at recess. They said it sounded really cool and they all wanted to buy it. I could see why. The commercial showed kids playing very exciting games.

The voice on TV boomed, "Light up your life with Moonbeam, the new video game system. Moonbeam is the only way you'll get to play the latest, greatest games. Don't be left in the stardust. Buy Moonbeam. Landing in stores soon!"

That was it. I had to have it. I love video games. And I did not want to be left in the stardust.

I headed straight for Daddy's office and poked my head in the door.

"May I ask you a question, Daddy? It will only take a minute," I said.

"A big minute, or a little minute?" asked Daddy. He was smiling.

"A medium-size minute," I replied. Then I asked my question. "There is a new video game system coming out. It is called Moonbeam. It looks very exciting and I would love to have it. Would you buy it for me? Please?" I asked.

I could tell my minute was up.

"I will think about it," replied Daddy. "Maybe I will get it for you for Christmas."

"Christmas? That is such a long time from now! Moonbeam will be landing in stores soon."

"I am sorry, Karen. We do not need a new game system. It can wait," said Daddy.

"But I want it *now*!" I groaned.

"I am sorry, Karen. My answer is no."

"May I please call Chicago? I have an important question to ask Mommy," I said.

"I know the question," Daddy said. "And the answer is no, you may not call Chicago to ask it."

"May I call Granny in Nebraska?" I asked. If at first you don't succeed, try and try again, right? Wrong.

"Absolutely not," replied Daddy.

Boo and bullfrogs. It was May. Christmas was in December. The *end* of December. That was nearly eight months away. I could not wait that long. I just could not.

Karen's Idea

When I left Daddy's office, I nearly smacked into David Michael.

"I heard what you were asking," he said. "I saw the commercial for Moonbeam too. It sounds so cool. I do not have enough money to buy it either."

Hmm. I was starting to get an idea.

"You do not have *enough* money. Does that mean you have *some* money?" I asked.

"I have saved up a lot. I have about half of what Moonbeam costs," said David Michael.

"That is good news!" I said. "I will be right back."

I ran upstairs to my room. I took out my savings and counted it carefully. It was nowhere near what David Michael had saved. But I was not going to let that stop me. I ran back downstairs.

"Here is my idea," I said. "Let's ask Daddy if you and I can buy Moonbeam together. That way we will not have to wait for Christmas."

"All right! I think we should ask him right now," said David Michael.

We knocked on Daddy's office door.

"May we come in?" I asked.

"Of course you can," replied Daddy.

"We do not want to wait until Christmas to get Moonbeam," said David Michael. "We want to get it as soon as it comes out."

"We want to buy it together," I said. "Is that okay with you?"

"I cannot see why not," said Daddy. "Do you each have enough money saved up?"

"I do!" replied David Michael. "I have enough for half."

"I do not have half yet. But I will," I replied. "I am going to get a job. What do you think of that?"

Daddy thought for a minute, then said, "I think it is a good idea, if you can handle the job responsibly."

"I will be the most responsible worker in Stoneybrook history," I replied.

"I guess that does it, then," said Daddy. "As soon as you have enough money, I will drive you two downtown to buy Moonbeam."

Yes! David Michael and I gave each other the thumbs-up sign.

"By the way, Karen," said Daddy. "What kind of job do you plan to get?"

Hmm. I had not thought about that yet. What kind of job could a seven-year-old get who needed to make money fast?

"Um, I will have to let you know," I replied. "I am sure I will have the answer for you right away."

Job Hunting

I went upstairs and flopped down on my bed with a pad of paper and a pencil. At the very top of a page I wrote in giant letters, "JOBS." Below that, I wrote a big number one.

"I need to think of a job I can do to earn money fast," I said to Moosie, my stuffed cat. "Do you have any ideas?"

I always know what Moosie is thinking. Now he was thinking about jobs I could do around the house. Such as dusting and watching Emily.

"I have done those kinds of jobs before," I said to Moosie. "They do not pay enough money. It would take me until Christmas to earn what I need. I do not want to wait that long."

I needed another kind of job. A job in the real world. A job that would pay a lot of money, and fast.

Maybe I would have to go to the library to get a book about jobs. Wait! Instead of getting a book, maybe I could *write* a book. I am a very good writer.

I wrote, "WRITE A BOOK" in big letters next to the number one on my list. I did not even have to write the number two. This was the job I wanted.

I turned to a fresh page in my pad. I was ready to write my book. All I had to do was decide what I wanted to write about. I tapped the pencil against my cheek and waited for an idea to come.

I had one idea after another, but none of them seemed right. Then I remembered when an author visited us at school. He said it sometimes takes a long time to get an idea you really want to work on. Then it can take a long time to write it the way you want.

But I did not have a long time. I wanted to make money right away. I decided being an author would have to wait. I needed to think of another way to make money.

I wrote a big number two on my list. In no time I had a new job idea. Next to the number two I wrote, "DETECTIVE."

Not long ago I found a map stuck in a wall at the little house. It was an old map and hard to follow. But with a little help from Kristy and Andrew, I found a hidden treasure in the backyard. It was a trunk filled with valuable coins.

But I did not find the treasure the first time I tried. Or the second. In fact, I dug up quite a bit of the backyard before finding the right place. Mommy and Seth were not too happy.

Maybe being a detective was not such a good plan.

I wrote a big number three on my list and

soon had another idea. I am very good at grooming horses. At pony camp, I got a prize for grooming my horse, Blueberry.

But there are not too many horses in Stoneybrook.

"I am not doing very well at this, Moosie," I said. "Job hunting is hard work. I want a raise!"

Wanted!

After dinner Nannie went into the den to read the paper. I remembered that Sam had looked at the want ads to find his job at the supermarket.

"Excuse me, Nannie. Are you through with the job page?" I asked.

Nannie knew that I needed to make money to buy Moonbeam with David Michael.

"You are welcome to the job page, Karen," she replied.

I took the page and plopped down on the couch. Then I popped up.

"I will be back," I said. "I need to get a pencil. I am sure there will be a lot of ads for me to circle."

I came back with a sharpened red pencil and started reading. But I was having a problem. Most of the ads were in some kind of code.

"Nannie, what is a *secy*?" I asked. "Is it a very hard job?"

"*Secy* is short for secretary," Nannie replied.

"Too bad," I said.

I could do some parts of a secretary's job very well. I am good at taking phone messages. (Well, most of the time. There have been times I have been in *big* trouble for not reporting important messages.) But I am not the best typist yet. So I did not circle the ad.

"What is an *oppty*?" I asked.

"Let me see," said Nannie. She looked at the place where I was pointing. It said, OPPTY OF A LIFETIME!

"That is short for opportunity," said Nannie.

I read on. The ad said the opportunity of a lifetime was to be an oil trucker for a big midwestern company. It sounded exciting, but not for me. I do not drive. I kept reading.

I came to an ad I could not understand at all. But I had to know what it said. It could be the perfect job.

"What is a *fincl resrchr*?" I asked.

Nannie looked at the page again.

"That means financial researcher."

"Why don't they spell these things the way they are supposed to?" I said. "I think the people who write these ads need to go back to second grade. They would learn how to be good spellers like me."

Nannie laughed. "Words that are shortened like these are called abbreviations. They take up less space in the newspaper so the ads cost less money."

"Well, I do not like them one bit," I said.

I decided to read only the ads that used whole words. That did not leave too many. I looked at one after another. In the very last column, an ad jumped out and called my name! It said:

WANTED
Delivery boys and girls
for a new community newspaper
printed three times a week.

I was so excited I could hardly sit still. Then I read the last line which was written in smaller print. It said:

Must be thirteen or older.

I did some fast math in my head and figured out I would have to wait six years before I could become a newspaper deliverer. Boo.

Teamwork

A few minutes later Kristy passed by the den. Suddenly I had a great idea.

I was already working as a team with David Michael to buy Moonbeam. Maybe I could work as a team with Kristy to deliver papers. Kristy is thirteen.

"See you later, Nannie," I said. "Thank you for helping me read the ads. I may have found the perfect job after all!"

I followed my big sister upstairs to her room. I knocked on the door.

"Come in," Kristy called.

"Guess what! I have an excellent oppty for you," I said.

"An excellent what?"

"Oppty. That is short for opportunity," I replied. "How would you like to make money delivering newspapers with me?"

"I am sorry, Karen. I do not think that would be a good idea," said Kristy. "I already have my schoolwork and baby-sitting jobs." (Kristy is the president of a baby-sitting business she runs with her friends.)

"But this will be so much fun. And it will not take much time. The paper only comes out three times a week."

"Really? That would not be too bad," said Kristy. "I can always use a little extra money."

"And you would not have to do the job by yourself. We could share the job and the money," I said.

"I think you are too young to deliver newspapers," said Kristy.

"I am not too young to fold them and put

32

on rubber bands. I could do that part of the job all by myself. Then we could deliver the papers together."

I could see that Kristy was starting to like the idea.

"You know who else could be on our team?" I said. "Scout."

Kristy's face brightened. She just loves our training-to-be-a-guide-dog puppy.

"Scout would love the extra morning walks," said Kristy.

"I have the ad right here. All we have to do is call the number to get more information," I said.

"It cannot hurt to have the information."

"Hooray!" I cried.

Kristy dialed the number. She found out how much the job paid. And what the paper route would be.

"This sounds very interesting," said Kristy. "Thank you for the information."

"What did they say?" I asked when Kristy hung up.

"You are right, Karen," said Kristy. "This job sounds pretty easy. It is three mornings a week. And the route is not very long."

"When can we start?" I asked.

"The person I spoke with said we can start this week. I will go to the office tomorrow and pick up an application."

"Yippee!"

I gave Kristy a big hug.

Bright and Early

The following afternoon Kristy brought home the application. We answered all the questions and then Daddy and Elizabeth signed the paper. Charlie drove us to the office, and our application was approved on the spot.

"You can begin tomorrow," said the man who hired us. "The papers will be dropped off at your house."

I was so excited. First I had to call my friends and tell them about my new job.

Then I had to pick out what I was going

to wear the next morning. I wanted an outfit I could put on *fast*. I did not want to get up any earlier than I had to. So I picked out sneakers that close with Velcro instead of laces. And I picked a shirt that slips over my head.

A little while later Kristy came in to say good night.

"Good night? It is only nine o'clock. You never go to bed so early," I said.

"I set my alarm clock for five tomorrow morning," replied Kristy. "That does not leave much time for sleeping. We do not want to be tired on our first day."

"I guess you are right," I said. "Good night. See you in the morning."

I decided to read a few pages in my mystery story to make me sleepy. But it turned out to be an exciting part. I had to keep turning the pages to see what happened. Finally I turned out the lights and went to sleep.

Bleep-bleep-bleep . . . bleep-bleep-bleep . . .

I opened my eyes. It was hardly light out. There had to be some mistake. No one could be expected to get up in the middle of the night to deliver newspapers.

I shut off my bleeping alarm clock and closed my eyes.

The next thing I knew, someone was shaking me awake.

"Karen! Karen, wake up!" said Kristy. "The newspapers are here. We have to get to work."

"I am on my way," I said. I rolled over.

"Karen, I am not kidding. Wake up!" said Kristy.

"All right," I replied. "I am getting up."

Kristy waited until I was out of bed and standing up before she left the room.

When I got downstairs, she had juice and a muffin waiting for me. I felt a little better after I ate.

"It is time to fold the papers. I have already done some for you," said Kristy.

We were supposed to fold each paper in thirds, then put on the rubber band. I folded one paper. Then another. My head started sinking lower and lower.

"Karen, do *not* fall asleep!" said Kristy.

"Sorry." I shook myself awake and folded some more papers. When we finished, a little pile of papers was in front of me and a big stack was in front of Kristy.

"Next time, you fold them all," Kristy said. "Folding was supposed to be your job."

It was time to deliver. I thought that would be the fun part. But my legs were not cooperating. I felt as if I had jelly knees. They hardly held me up. I watched Scout race out of the house. I wondered where she got her energy. I wished she could give a little of it to me.

"Could you walk a little faster, please?" said Kristy. "At this rate we will never get finished."

"I am right behind you!" I said.

I did a sleepwalk shuffle up one street and down the next. My sack of papers grew lighter as we walked along. Finally the last paper was gone.

Picky, Picky!

On Thursday night I got into bed at nine o'clock on the dot. I did not want to be as tired on my second day of delivering papers as I was on my first.

I was just drifting off when I heard the telephone ring. At first I thought my alarm clock was ringing. I pushed the off button. Then I heard Elizabeth talking.

"I think Karen has already gone to bed," she said.

I popped up and called, "I am not asleep

yet!" I did not want to miss an exciting phone call.

It turned out to be Natalie Springer, who is in my class. She had a question about our math homework. The call was not exciting. But it was enough to wake me up.

I went back to bed. After a long time I fell asleep. The next thing I knew, Kristy was shaking me.

"Wake up!" she said.

"What happened? I did not hear my clock," I replied.

Uh-oh. I remembered turning it off when the phone rang the night before. I forgot to reset it.

"I will get dressed extra fast," I said.

I tried. But first I put my shirt on backward. I had to take it off and put it on again. Then I could not find my socks. Finally I found them stuffed in my sneakers. (I had put them there so they would be easy to find.)

Most of the papers were already folded

and banded by the time I got downstairs. Kristy gave me a Look.

"Sorry," I said.

I gobbled my breakfast, then followed Kristy and Scout out the door.

At the fourth house on our paper route, we saw a man standing on his porch.

"Excuse me," he said. "May I speak with you?"

"Of course," said Kristy. "We hope you are happy with your paper delivery."

"The truth is, I could be a little happier," replied the man. "I will tell you exactly how I like my paper delivered."

"Karen, I put a notepad and pen in our paper sack. Please be sure to write this down so we do not forget anything," said Kristy. Kristy is very organized.

I found the pad and pen and started writing. The man had a lot of instructions. He wanted his paper delivered headline up and facing toward the house. That way he could read it just by looking out the window. He also wanted his paper placed gently on the porch and never tossed because it might hit the door and wake him if he slept late. I wrote this down as fast as I could.

The next few houses were quiet. Then we saw a woman holding a little dog in her arms.

"Good morning," said the woman. "I have been waiting to talk to you."

The woman did not look very happy.

"Frisco ate my paper on Wednesday," she said.

"We are sorry," replied Kristy.

"Yes, well, you did not know," said the woman. "From now on, please put my newspaper in the box on my lawn. That way Frisco cannot get his little teeth into it."

"Of course," said Kristy. She turned to me. "Karen? Are you writing this down?"

"Every word," I replied. I smiled at the woman. I was too sleepy to have a conversation. (When I am awake, I am usually *very* talkative.)

Three more people were waiting for us with special instructions. Two more called us after we got home. There were a lot of instructions to write down. When it came to having papers delivered, some people were picky, picky!

A Mysterious Friend

On Saturday morning I opened my eyes and popped up in bed.

I have to get up, I thought. I cannot be late.

I shook myself awake. Then I remembered there was no weekend edition of the newspaper. I was free! My head dropped back to the pillow. I was asleep in no time.

I slept a lot over the weekend. It felt so good. There was only one problem. I got so caught up on my sleep that I was not tired on Sunday night. But I needed to go to sleep early so I could get up for work on Monday.

I got into bed at nine o'clock. I tossed and turned for hours. When my clock went off on Monday morning, I dragged myself out of bed and started to dress. I was gigundoly tired. But I did not want Kristy to be upset with me. I was almost ready when she poked her head into my room.

"I am glad to see you are up, Karen," she said. "Be sure to bring the notepad with everyone's instructions."

I went downstairs with the notepad in my pocket. Kristy and I folded and banded the papers. We ate breakfast. Then we headed out the door.

"Please read our first special instruction," said Kristy.

I opened the pad. What I had written looked like this:

"Um, I am having a little trouble making out what I wrote," I said. "Maybe you can read it."

I passed the notepad to Kristy. She looked at one page, then flipped to the next. And the next.

"Karen! These notes are a mess!" she said.

"I guess I was writing too fast," I replied. "Do not worry. If we deliver the papers the wrong way, people will call and tell us."

"I bet they will!" said Kristy. "They will also be very angry."

She stomped ahead. I had to run to catch up.

Together we remembered most of the instructions. At one house Kristy put the paper headline up and not too close to the door. A few houses down, she put the paper in the box on the lawn so the dog could not get it.

I thought we were doing pretty well. Then we came to a house where we were sure there had been no special instructions. We had never seen or heard from the person who lived there. As we got closer, we saw the shadow of a woman at the window.

"Maybe she has instructions for us today," I said to Kristy. "I promise to write neatly so we can read them."

But the shadow quickly disappeared.

"I did not think this woman would talk to us," said Kristy. "In fact, I am surprised we deliver papers to her house at all. I did not think she was interested in community news. She keeps to herself."

Kristy handed me a paper. I hurried up the porch steps and placed the paper by the door. On the way back, I noticed a little package sitting on the window ledge. It was tied with red ribbon. A tag hanging from it said, FOR NEWSPAPER DELIVERERS.

Hmm. What was it? I picked up the package and looked back at the window. No one was there. I ran to the street. Kristy was already heading to the next house.

"Kristy, look! I found this on the woman's porch," I said.

"Let's see what it is. Open it," said Kristy.

I untied the ribbon. Inside was a sealed package with two granola bars in it.

"She left us breakfast!" I exclaimed.

"That is a mysterious thing to do."

"I think it is a nice thing to do!" I said. "She wants to be our friend."

Ribbons or
Rubber Bands?

Our next delivery day was Wednesday. When the alarm went off at five o'clock, I was as tired as ever. But I got out of bed fast anyway. I was thinking about our mysterious new friend. I wondered if she would leave another goody for Kristy and me.

"Wow! You are already dressed!" said Kristy when she peeked in my door. "Come on. You can start folding and banding while I get some breakfast ready."

"I will be down in a minute," I replied.

I had thought of something I needed to do

first. It was the right and friendly thing to do. I found a piece of paper and my favorite purple marker. I wrote a thank-you note to our new friend. It said:

THANK YOU FOR THE GRANOLA BARS. WE DO GET HUNGRY BY THE END OF OUR PAPER ROUTE. WE ATE THEM AS SOON AS WE GOT HOME. THEY WERE EXCELLENT!
YOUR NEW FRIEND, KAREN

(I did not tell her we had had to wait to ask Daddy's permission to eat the bars. But we did. We are not allowed to eat food from strangers unless a grown-up at our house says it is okay.)

By the time I got downstairs, Kristy was angry.

"Karen Brewer, I do not understand you!" she said. "You were already up and dressed and you are *still* late. I am almost finished folding the papers."

"I am sorry. I wanted to write a thank-you

note to the person who gave us the present," I replied. "It is the polite thing to do, and I wanted our customer to be happy."

"Our customers will be happy if they get their papers on time," said Kristy. "Please eat your breakfast so we can go."

I ate my breakfast in record time, and we were out the door with minutes to spare.

I could not wait to finish the first part of our paper route. I decided that delivering papers was pretty boring. Unless you have a new friend who leaves you a present every now and then.

I raced up the stairs to our friend's porch. I had a paper and a thank-you note to deliver.

Guess what! Another package was waiting for us. I hurried down the stairs to show Kristy.

"Well, we do seem to have a new friend," Kristy said. "Let's see what she gave us today."

I tore open the paper. Inside were two tortoiseshell barrettes.

"I cannot believe this! What great presents," I said.

By the time I got home, I decided a note would not be enough of a thank-you for our friend. I wanted to give her something in return. At school we were making origami animals. (Origami is the art of Japanese paper folding.) A beautiful paper bird would be the perfect gift for our new friend.

On Thursday night I wrapped the bird carefully in tissue paper. But when I got up on Friday morning and looked at it, I knew the gift was not right. It did not look pretty enough. I decided to tie some colored ribbons on the package.

"Karen, what are you doing?" said Kristy, poking her head into my room.

"I was just tying some ribbons on the gift for our friend. Will you sign a note if I write one?" I asked.

"There is no time for notes and no time for ribbons! We have papers to deliver. But first we have to fold and band them."

"I will be right down," I said.

"I have heard that one before," said Kristy. And she disappeared downstairs.

I knew it was not nice of me to let Kristy do all the work. But tying ribbons on presents was much more fun than putting rubber bands on newspapers. And Kristy is an excellent big sister. I was sure she would forgive me.

The Rules

Kristy forgave me.

"But please do not do it again," she said. "Remember, we are a team. That is what you said when we took this job together."

"You are right. I promise to be a good teammate from now on," I replied.

On Monday school was closed because of a teacher meeting. I was happy to have the day off. I needed my rest.

When I went to sleep Sunday night, I did not set my clock. I planned to sleep until I could not sleep anymore.

But the next morning someone shook me awake. It was Kristy.

"Karen, what are you doing?" she asked.

"I am sleeping. I have today off," I said.

"You have the day off from *school*, not from *work*! The papers must be delivered."

"But . . . but . . ." I said. My eyes were still half closed.

"No buts! Get out of bed this minute!"

"Oh, all right." I groaned. "I am coming."

I did not get ready too fast. I was not about to rush on my day off. As long as I was working, though, I wanted to leave something for my friend.

I found a pencil I had not used yet. I rolled it up in paper and drew a heart on the outside of the package.

By the time I was downstairs, Kristy was fighting mad. She had folded and banded all the papers. It was so late that she said there was no time for me to eat breakfast. My stomach was rumbling. Boo.

I was too hungry and tired to rush. I could not keep up with Kristy and Scout.

That set us behind even more.

When we reached our mysterious friend's house, a package was waiting for us. Kristy would not let me stop to open it.

"We have to get back to the house," she said. "I have to go to school even if you do not!"

I raced to put my present on my friend's porch. But I worried that I had put it in a place where it could be missed. I ran back to move it.

We were so late that Kristy missed the school bus. She had to ask Daddy for a ride.

"This afternoon, we are going to have a meeting and make some rules!" she said as she ran out the door.

When Kristy came home from school she handed me a sheet of paper that said:

PAPER ROUTE RULES
Each employee must . . .
- Be on time or lose pay!
- Fold and band half the papers.

- Be cheerful and considerate at all times.

"And from now on we will deliver the papers on our bicycles. It will be a whole lot faster," said Kristy.

I promised to follow the rules. And riding my bicycle sounded like fun. On Wednesday morning we tried out our new system.

I was up on time. I folded and banded half the papers. I tried my best to be cheerful and considerate. And I followed along on my bicycle.

"Come on, Karen. You can ride faster than that!" said Kristy.

I was lagging behind.

"My legs are shorter than yours. They do not take me as far," I whined.

Oops. I was not being cheerful. And I was slowing us down. Kristy could not ride ahead because she had to watch out for me. Especially when we needed to cross a street.

I pedaled as fast as I could. But it was not fast enough.

"This is not working out at all," said Kristy. "I don't know what we are going to do."

I did not have any ideas either. I was too tired to think.

A for Effort

I was tired most of the time. I was too tired to play outside with my friends. I was too tired to stay up and talk on the phone. I was too tired to do much of anything.

On Thursday afternoon I was in my room trying to stay awake so I could do my homework. But my eyes were closing and my head kept dropping down into my notebook.

Maybe this job is not worth it, I thought. I used to have energy. I used to have fun. But I am not having much fun anymore.

There was a noise in my room that was

making me cranky. It was a noise I had heard lots of times before. It was Emily Junior running on the wheel inside her cage. Now that I was tired, it sounded like the worst and loudest noise in the world.

I had not finished my homework, but I had to get out of my room. I went downstairs. Sam was in the den watching TV. He looked even crankier than me.

"Why are you here, instead of at work?" I asked.

"I was fired," said Sam. "The store decided they had too many part-time workers."

"That is not fair!" I said.

Now I had something important to be cranky about.

Sam just shrugged and stared at the TV. I sat there keeping him company. While I was sitting, I thought, what if I lost *my* job? What if I overslept again? What if I was too tired to be cheerful? Maybe Kristy would fire me!

I did not love my job, but I *needed* it. I

needed it to buy Moonbeam. I would have to try to be an excellent worker.

"Excuse me, Sam," I said. "I am very sorry to hear about your job. But I have to do my homework now."

"Okay. Thanks, Karen," said Sam.

I had to finish my homework soon. Otherwise I would need to stay up late. Then I would be too tired to get up the next morning. And Friday was paper-route day!

I shook myself awake every time I felt like nodding off. My homework was finished by dinnertime.

After dinner, I drew a beautiful picture to give to my mysterious friend. This is how I signed it:

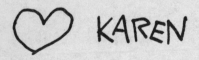

I was washed and ready for bed by quarter of nine. That was fifteen minutes earlier than usual on a work night. I wanted to have plenty of time to fall asleep.

I turned off the lights and closed my eyes. Instead of counting sheep, I counted moonbeams. "One moonbeam. Two moonbeams. Three moonbeams."

I must have fallen asleep right away. I do not even remember counting to ten.

In the morning I was up and out of bed as soon as my alarm clock went off. I dressed quickly and ran downstairs. I was there before Kristy.

I brought in the papers and started folding and banding them. By the time Kristy arrived, I already had a neat pile of papers in front of me.

"Karen? Is that really you?" asked my sister, rubbing her eyes.

"It sure is," I replied proudly.

Kristy smiled.

"This is not my favorite job in the world. Getting up so early is really hard," she said. "But when you help out, it is a whole lot easier."

"I am going to try hard from now on," I promised.

"Today you get an *A* for effort," said Kristy.

"Next time I want an *A* plus!" I replied.

There She Is!

When we reached our mysterious friend's house, I put the drawing I had made under a flowerpot on the porch.

(Kristy said she appreciated the gifts but did not have time to make any in return.)

I looked at the window ledge. Then I looked below it. There was nothing in either place. First I felt bad. Then I felt worried. A gift had been waiting every newspaper delivery day since we got our granola bars.

Then I saw them. About a foot away from

the window were two tulips tied with ribbons. One was red tied with a yellow ribbon. The other was yellow tied with a red ribbon.

I looked up toward the window.

"Thank you," I said in case anyone was listening.

The next day Nannie was making strawberries dipped in her secret Chocolate Magic sauce.

"Is there any chance you will have extra chocolate strawberries?" I asked. "I know someone who might like them."

"Might that someone be you?" asked Nannie.

"No, it is for a friend on my paper route," I replied.

"Oh, who is that?"

I told Nannie the address.

Nannie thought for a minute. Then she said, "That is Mrs. Casper. I have not seen her since her husband died. She always seemed like a nice person."

"She leaves gifts for Kristy and me," I told Nannie. "And I have been leaving gifts for her."

"I will be sure to save a few strawberries," said Nannie. "I am glad you have a nice new friend."

I made a tinfoil tent for the strawberries and tied colored ribbons on top. I left my gift on Monday. Another gift was waiting for Kristy and me: two refrigerator magnets shaped like newspapers.

On Wednesday, I brought a funny cartoon in a homemade frame as my gift. (It was a *Peanuts* cartoon from the paper.)

I was better about getting up in the morning, so we left the house earlier than usual.

Our friend probably did not expect us to arrive as early as we did. When we turned the corner, we saw her on her porch!

"Look, Kristy! There she is!" I said.

But by the time Kristy looked up, she was already gone.

I had been too far away to see her face. But I could see she was wearing tan slacks and a white shirt. She looked like a regular person.

But if Mrs. Casper was a regular person, why had she disappeared so fast? Was she hiding from us?

Our friend was still a mystery.

A Miserable Morning

It was raining when I woke up on Friday. Our papers came late. They also came with a supply of plastic bags. We were supposed to slip the papers into the bags so they would not get wet. That meant we had to fold, band, and bag the papers. There was no way we could do that and still leave on time.

We were working as fast as we could when we noticed Shannon wrestling with something on the floor.

Grrr! Woof! Grrr! Woof!

She was playing with . . .

"Oh, no!" cried Kristy.

Kristy gently pried the newspaper away from the dog.

"We always get a couple of extra papers in case of emergencies, right?" I asked.

"Yes, but now we have only one extra," said Kristy. "We have to keep an eye on that dog!"

Thanks to Shannon, we were even more behind than before.

"I cannot be late for school today," said Kristy. "I have to take a test."

"I need to eat breakfast," I said. "Last time I went out without breakfast, I felt sick."

I poured myself a bowl of cereal and ate it in four bites. As soon as I finished, I was sorry.

"Ugh. Now I have a stomachache." I moaned.

"Eat a piece of bread. That might settle your stomach," said Kristy.

She was still working on the papers.

I munched on a piece of bread. It worked. I felt a little bit better.

Kristy stuffed the last paper into the last plastic bag.

"I am exhausted. And we have not even started delivering yet," said Kristy.

"I am exhausted too. We need help."

Kristy and I looked at each other. We must have had the same idea at the same time.

"Do you think they would do it?" I asked.

I did not have to say who "they" were. I was sure Kristy knew.

"They will not like getting up at this hour," she said.

"This is a desperate situation," I replied. (I had heard a detective say that on a TV show once. I have wanted to use that line ever since.)

"You are right," said Kristy. "If we are going to ask for help, we had better do it now."

Kristy and I ran upstairs together. We each knocked on a door. We had no idea what was going to happen next.

Sam and Charlie
to the Rescue

"Huh?" said Sam. "Is it six-thirty already?"

"No. It is five-thirty," I replied.

"Five-thirty in the afternoon? Was I napping?"

"No. It is five-thirty in the morning. You were fast asleep," I replied.

Sam opened his eyes.

"If I was sleeping, why am I awake?"

"I woke you up to ask a favor," I said. "Well, not really a favor. We will pay you."

I explained about the paper route and how late we were.

"Oh, all right. Now that I lost my job, I could use the money," Sam replied.

Charlie agreed also. The four of us were out the door in ten minutes. Thank goodness the rain had stopped.

While we were delivering papers, I was thinking. I was thinking about delivering papers. I decided to make a list in my head of the good things and the bad things about the job. First I thought about the bad things:

Getting up and going to sleep early.
Missing my friends because I am too tired to play and cannot talk on the phone at night.
Feeling tired most of the time.

Then I thought of the good things:

Making money.
Having a new friend.
Getting and giving gifts.

Hmm. I added up in my head how much money I had made. It was already enough for my share of Moonbeam. I crossed "Making money" off the list. That left only two reasons to keep the job: my friend and the gifts.

I was thinking about my friend when we arrived at her house. I took the gift I had made for her out of my pocket. I had written a poem and drawn a picture:

A TULIP FOR KRISTY,
A TULIP FOR ME.
HERE'S A TULIP FOR YOU,
AND THAT WILL MAKE THREE.

I ran to the porch. Our gifts were waiting on the window ledge. Mrs. Casper was very thoughtful. She had wrapped the gifts in plastic because of the rain. Here is what they were: two tiny address books with flowered covers.

How could I stop delivering papers? I would miss giving gifts. I would miss getting gifts. And even though I did not see her, I would miss my friend.

I knew she would miss me too.

A Big Relief

We were almost finished with our paper route. There were just a few more houses to go. Thanks to Sam and Charlie, all the papers would be delivered on time.

When we were finally finished and on the way home, I looked at Kristy. She was yawning.

Then I looked at Sam and Charlie. They seemed fine. Especially Sam. He was even joking around.

"What newspaper do cows like to read?" he asked.

We all gave up.

"*The Daily Moos!*"

I could not believe I did not get the answer. I have heard that joke a hundred times. I must have been really tired.

But I was not too tired to have a good idea. Sam was great at this job. And he needed a job, because he had lost his. My idea was to ask Sam to deliver the papers.

I did not want to be a quitter. But sometimes you have to make a choice. Sometimes something you thought would be great turns out not to be great for you. Then stopping is not about being a quitter. It is about being smart.

I knew Kristy had not wanted this job to begin with. She would be happy to give it up. And I did not want to disappoint Mrs. Casper. But I would find a way to explain it to her.

I wanted to ask Sam then and there about taking the job. But Kristy and I were a team. I decided to be a good team player and ask her about my idea first. I thought this was very grown-up.

Kristy did not have time to hear my idea when we got home. I had to be very grown-up and wait a little longer.

Just before dinner I got my chance to talk to Kristy.

"Here is my idea," I said. "I do not think you really like delivering papers."

"You are right about that," said Kristy.

"I do not like the job either. And I already have enough money to buy Moonbeam with David Michael. But Sam needs to make money. He was very unhappy about losing his job at the A&P. I think this job would be perfect for him. But I did not want to say anything to him until I asked my team-mate."

"That was very grown-up of you, Karen. And I like your idea a lot," replied Kristy. "You know, once you started following the rules, working with you was really fun. I am glad we took this job together. But now I will be glad to say good-bye to it. And the sooner the better!"

"We can talk to Sam right now — as a team," I said.

We found Sam napping in the den. I gently shook him awake.

"Huh? What time is it?" he said.

"Five-thirty," I replied.

"No! Not again!"

"No, it is five-thirty in the afternoon. You were taking a nap."

When Sam was completely awake, we told him our idea.

"Sounds great," he replied. "I do not like getting up so early. But once I am up, I am okay. And I really could use the money."

"Then it is done," said Kristy. "I will call the newspaper office and we can tell them about the switch."

Kristy and I gave each other the thumbs-up sign. Our newspaper delivery days were over. It was a big relief!

Mrs. Casper

There was one more thing I had to do. I had to explain everything to Mrs. Casper.

After dinner, I went upstairs and wrote a note on my best stationery. It said:

DEAR MRS. CASPER,

YOU HAVE BEEN A WONDERFUL NEW FRIEND — EVEN THOUGH WE HAVE NOT MET! THANK YOU FOR THE BEAUTIFUL GIFTS.

I HAVE SOME NEWS. KRISTY AND I WILL NOT BE DELIVERING YOUR NEWSPAPER ANYMORE. IT IS HARD FOR US TO GO TO SCHOOL AND HAVE A MORN-

ING JOB. MY BROTHER SAM, WHO IS OLDER, WILL
BE DELIVERING YOUR PAPERS FROM NOW ON.

♡ KAREN BREWER

I wanted to tell Mrs. Casper that if she
had any more gifts for me she could leave
them for Sam to pick up. But I did not want
to sound greedy. I put my note in an enve-
lope and drew a bouquet of flowers on the
outside.

On Tuesday after school Kristy and I delivered my note. The house looked extra
quiet in the bright sunlight. At other houses
you could hear voices coming from inside.
Doors were opening and closing.

Guess what. As I was slipping my note
under the flowerpot, Mrs. Casper's door
opened! I jumped back. Mrs. Casper was my
friend, but she was still mysterious. I was a
little afraid.

Until I saw her face. It was a friendly
face with a big smile. I wondered what had
made her open the door.

"Karen? Are you all right? You are not usually here at this time," she said.

Now I *knew* she was nice. She had come outside because she was worried about me.

"I am fine," I replied. "I was just leaving you a note to tell you that Kristy and I will not be delivering your newspaper anymore."

"Would you girls like to come inside for some lemonade?" asked Mrs. Casper. "A note is nice, but a real visit is even nicer."

Since Nannie knew Mrs. Casper, I thought it would be all right to go inside. I looked at Kristy to see if she thought it was okay too. Kristy nodded.

"Thank you," we said to Mrs. Casper.

We waited in the living room while Mrs. Casper fixed the lemonade. The house was cozy and friendly. And my gifts were everywhere! The origami bird was on the windowsill. The cartoon was on the coffee table. The tulip poem was on the mantel over the fireplace. I felt very proud.

"Yes, your gifts are all around," said Mrs.

Casper, returning with the lemonade and cookies. "I love each and every one of them."

"We love your gifts too," said Kristy. "Thank you very much."

"I'm wearing the barrette you gave me," I said. I turned my head so she could see it.

"It looks very pretty on you," said Mrs. Casper.

While we drank our lemonade, we told Mrs. Casper why we would not be delivering her newspaper anymore.

"I understand. It is hard to get up so early," said Mrs. Casper. "But I will miss seeing you."

"I could come visit sometimes," I said.

"I would love that. Since my husband died, I do not get out as much as I used to. You are my first new friends."

It would be fun visiting Mrs. Casper, because I liked her. It would be nice too, because then she would not feel so lonely.

On our way out, Mrs. Casper gave us each a bag of cookies.

"Thank you," said Kristy.

"I did not expect you today, so I'm sorry I do not have a real gift," said Mrs. Casper.

"I *love* gifts," I replied. "But you do not have to give me gifts all the time. Being friends is enough for me."

Moonbeam

A few days later Nannie was in the den reading the paper. David Michael and I were each reading a book.

"Here is an ad for Moonbeam. Is that what you two were going to buy?" asked Nannie.

"Yes!" I replied. "Is it out yet?"

"It will be in the stores tomorrow."

David Michael and I jumped up and raced to find Daddy.

"Tomorrow is Saturday and Moonbeam

is going to be in the stores," said David Michael.

"Would you drive us downtown to buy it?" I asked. "Please?"

"I sure will," said Daddy. "I am proud of you two for finding a way to buy it together."

The next morning we were the first customers at Toy City.

"Look, we can try it out," said David Michael. A demonstration model of Moonbeam was on display.

We turned it on and selected a game for two players called Space Walkers. Asteroids were shooting all around. The space walkers had to reach their ship without being hit.

The screen was filled with bright colors. The asteroids seemed to be shooting right off the screen! There was exciting music too. David Michael and I were jumping up and down and yelling.

"Calm down, kids," said Daddy.

Just then a salesman stepped up to us. I

thought he was going to ask us to keep our voices down. But he did not.

"I am glad to see you are enjoying Moonbeam. It is a terrific new system," he said. "Do you have any questions?"

"How many games does it come with?" I asked.

"It comes with three games, and you can buy others. We have one new game in stock already," said the salesman.

"What game is it?" asked David Michael.

"How much does it cost?" I asked.

"It is in the stockroom. We have not even unpacked it yet," said the salesman. "I will get it and be right back."

We tried another game called Road Racers while we waited. It was fun too. Then the salesman came back.

"Here it is," he said. "The game is called Paper Route. It costs twenty-nine dollars and ninety-five cents."

"Paper Route! I need that game!" I said.

David Michael studied the box.

"It looks great," he said.

There was only one problem. A big problem. We did not have enough money to buy it. But I had an idea.

"May we exchange this game for one of the others?" I asked.

"I am sorry," said the salesman. "No substitutions."

Boo. Now I would have to take another job. I wondered if Sam needed my help delivering papers.

"Hold on," said Daddy. "Since you did such a good job raising the money for Moonbeam yourselves, I would like to buy the extra game for you."

"Thank you!" said David Michael and I together.

I gave Daddy a big hug. Then I thought of something.

"Before we buy it, I would like to read the instructions," I said.

"I am sure it is not hard to play," said David Michael.

"I need to check one thing," I replied.

I read the instructions from start to finish. Then I said, "We will take it!"

"What was that about?" asked Daddy.

"Since the game is called Paper Route, I wanted to be sure we would not have to get up early to play it," I said.

After we had paid for everything, we headed home. I felt proud of myself. I had made a plan with David Michael and carried it out. I had worked hard to become a good paper-route teammate with Kristy. And I had made a new friend.

Hmm. I wondered if Mrs. Casper liked to play video games. On my next visit, I would be sure to ask her.

L. GODWIN

About the Author

ANN M. MARTIN lives in New York City and loves animals, especially cats. She has two cats of her own, Gussie and Woody.

Other books by Ann M. Martin that you might enjoy are *Stage Fright*; *Me and Katie (the Pest)*; and the books in *The Baby-sitters Club* series.

Ann likes ice cream and *I Love Lucy*. And she has her own little sister, whose name is Jane.

Little Sister

Don't miss #98

KAREN'S FISHING TRIP

"I have an idea," I said softly.

"Uh-oh," groaned Nancy. "Sometimes your ideas mean trouble."

Hannie giggled. I knew Nancy was just teasing me.

"Listen," I said. "Every morning we will be going out on the dock to practice fishing, right? So from now on, I will take a camera with me. If there is a Lake Monster, sooner or later it will have to come up for air. I will be right there with my camera. And I can be the first person to get a picture of the monster! We can all be famous!"

"That is a pretty good plan," said Nancy reluctantly.

"I think we should do it," said Hannie.

"Okay," I said. "Tomorrow I will bring my camera."

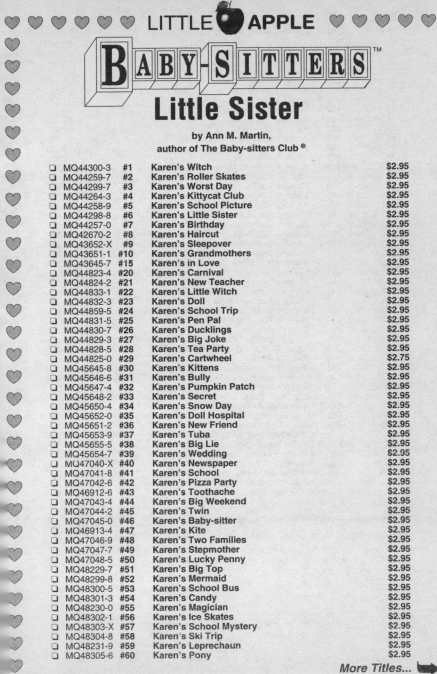

LITTLE APPLE

BABY-SITTERS™
Little Sister

by Ann M. Martin,
author of The Baby-sitters Club ®

❏ MQ44300-3	#1	Karen's Witch	$2.95
❏ MQ44259-7	#2	Karen's Roller Skates	$2.95
❏ MQ44299-7	#3	Karen's Worst Day	$2.95
❏ MQ44264-3	#4	Karen's Kittycat Club	$2.95
❏ MQ44258-9	#5	Karen's School Picture	$2.95
❏ MQ44298-8	#6	Karen's Little Sister	$2.95
❏ MQ44257-0	#7	Karen's Birthday	$2.95
❏ MQ42670-2	#8	Karen's Haircut	$2.95
❏ MQ43652-X	#9	Karen's Sleepover	$2.95
❏ MQ43651-1	#10	Karen's Grandmothers	$2.95
❏ MQ43645-7	#15	Karen's in Love	$2.95
❏ MQ44823-4	#20	Karen's Carnival	$2.95
❏ MQ44824-2	#21	Karen's New Teacher	$2.95
❏ MQ44833-1	#22	Karen's Little Witch	$2.95
❏ MQ44832-3	#23	Karen's Doll	$2.95
❏ MQ44859-5	#24	Karen's School Trip	$2.95
❏ MQ44831-5	#25	Karen's Pen Pal	$2.95
❏ MQ44830-7	#26	Karen's Ducklings	$2.95
❏ MQ44829-3	#27	Karen's Big Joke	$2.95
❏ MQ44828-5	#28	Karen's Tea Party	$2.95
❏ MQ44825-0	#29	Karen's Cartwheel	$2.75
❏ MQ45645-8	#30	Karen's Kittens	$2.95
❏ MQ45646-6	#31	Karen's Bully	$2.95
❏ MQ45647-4	#32	Karen's Pumpkin Patch	$2.95
❏ MQ45648-2	#33	Karen's Secret	$2.95
❏ MQ45650-4	#34	Karen's Snow Day	$2.95
❏ MQ45652-0	#35	Karen's Doll Hospital	$2.95
❏ MQ45651-2	#36	Karen's New Friend	$2.95
❏ MQ45653-9	#37	Karen's Tuba	$2.95
❏ MQ45655-5	#38	Karen's Big Lie	$2.95
❏ MQ45654-7	#39	Karen's Wedding	$2.95
❏ MU47040-X	#40	Karen's Newspaper	$2.95
❏ MQ47041-8	#41	Karen's School	$2.95
❏ MQ47042-6	#42	Karen's Pizza Party	$2.95
❏ MQ46912-6	#43	Karen's Toothache	$2.95
❏ MQ47043-4	#44	Karen's Big Weekend	$2.95
❏ MQ47044-2	#45	Karen's Twin	$2.95
❏ MQ47045-0	#46	Karen's Baby-sitter	$2.95
❏ MQ46913-4	#47	Karen's Kite	$2.95
❏ MQ47046-9	#48	Karen's Two Families	$2.95
❏ MQ47047-7	#49	Karen's Stepmother	$2.95
❏ MQ47048-5	#50	Karen's Lucky Penny	$2.95
❏ MQ48229-7	#51	Karen's Big Top	$2.95
❏ MQ48299-8	#52	Karen's Mermaid	$2.95
❏ MQ48300-5	#53	Karen's School Bus	$2.95
❏ MQ48301-3	#54	Karen's Candy	$2.95
❏ MQ48230-0	#55	Karen's Magician	$2.95
❏ MQ48302-1	#56	Karen's Ice Skates	$2.95
❏ MQ48303-X	#57	Karen's School Mystery	$2.95
❏ MQ48304-8	#58	Karen's Ski Trip	$2.95
❏ MQ48231-9	#59	Karen's Leprechaun	$2.95
❏ MQ48305-6	#60	Karen's Pony	$2.95

More Titles... ➡

The Baby-sitters Little Sister titles continued...

❑ MQ48306-4	#61	Karen's Tattletale	$2.95
❑ MQ48307-2	#62	Karen's New Bike	$2.95
❑ MQ25996-2	#63	Karen's Movie	$2.95
❑ MQ25997-0	#64	Karen's Lemonade Stand	$2.95
❑ MQ25998-9	#65	Karen's Toys	$2.95
❑ MQ26279-3	#66	Karen's Monsters	$2.95
❑ MQ26024-3	#67	Karen's Turkey Day	$2.95
❑ MQ26025-1	#68	Karen's Angel	$2.95
❑ MQ26193-2	#69	Karen's Big Sister	$2.95
❑ MQ26280-7	#70	Karen's Grandad	$2.95
❑ MQ26194-0	#71	Karen's Island Adventure	$2.95
❑ MQ26195-9	#72	Karen's New Puppy	$2.95
❑ MQ26301-3	#73	Karen's Dinosaur	$2.95
❑ MQ26214-9	#74	Karen's Softball Mystery	$2.95
❑ MQ69183-X	#75	Karen's County Fair	$2.95
❑ MQ69184-8	#76	Karen's Magic Garden	$2.95
❑ MQ69185-6	#77	Karen's School Surprise	$2.99
❑ MQ69186-4	#78	Karen's Half Birthday	$2.99
❑ MQ69187-2	#79	Karen's Big Fight	$2.99
❑ MQ69188-0	#80	Karen's Christmas Tree	$2.99
❑ MQ69189-9	#81	Karen's Accident	$2.99
❑ MQ69190-2	#82	Karen's Secret Valentine	$3.50
❑ MQ69191-0	#83	Karen's Bunny	$3.50
❑ MQ69192-9	#84	Karen's Big Job	$3.50
❑ MQ69193-7	#85	Karen's Treasure	$3.50
❑ MQ69194-5	#86	Karen's Telephone Trouble	$3.50
❑ MQ06585-8	#87	Karen's Pony Camp	$3.50
❑ MQ06586-6	#88	Karen's Puppet Show	$3.50
❑ MQ06587-4	#89	Karen's Unicorn	$3.50
❑ MQ06588-2	#90	Karen's Haunted House	$3.50
❑ MQ06589-0	#91	Karen's Pilgrim	$3.50
❑ MQ06590-4	#92	Karen's Sleigh Ride	$3.50
❑ MQ06591-2	#93	Karen's Cooking Contest	$3.50
❑ MQ06592-0	#94	Karen's Snow Princess	$3.50
❑ MQ06593-9	#95	Karen's Promise	$3.50
❑ MQ06594-7	#96	Karen's Big Move	$3.50
❑ MQ06595-5	#97	Karen's Paper Route	$3.50
❑ MQ55407-7		BSLS Jump Rope Pack	$5.99
❑ MQ73914-X		BSLS Playground Games Pack	$5.99
❑ MQ89735-7		BSLS Photo Scrapbook Book and Camera Pack	$9.99
❑ MQ47677-7		BSLS School Scrapbook	$2.95
❑ MQ43647-3		Karen's Wish Super Special #1	$3.25
❑ MQ44834-X		Karen's Plane Trip Super Special #2	$3.25
❑ MQ44827-7		Karen's Mystery Super Special #3	$3.25
❑ MQ45644-X		Karen, Hannie, and Nancy The Three Musketeers Super Special #4	$2.95
❑ MQ45649-0		Karen's Baby Super Special #5	$3.50
❑ MQ46911-8		Karen's Campout Super Special #6	$3.25

Available wherever you buy books, or use this order form.

Scholastic Inc., P.O. Box 7502, 2931 E. McCarty Street, Jefferson City, MO 65102

Please send me the books I have checked above. I am enclosing $_____
(please add $2.00 to cover shipping and handling). Send check or money order – no
cash or C.O.Ds please.

Name_____ Birthdate _____

Address_____

City_____ State/Zip _____

Please allow four to six weeks for delivery. Offer good in U.S.A. only. Sorry, mail orders are not
available to residents of Canada. Prices subject to change.   BLS1097